CUENTO DE LUZ

To Mateo, Andrea, and Emilia.
— Ignacio Sanz —

To Moi, Candela, and Mateo, my everything.
— Eva Poyato —

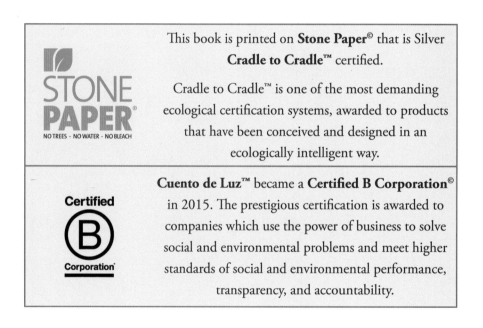

STONE PAPER®
NO TREES - NO WATER - NO BLEACH

This book is printed on **Stone Paper©** that is Silver **Cradle to Cradle™** certified.

Cradle to Cradle™ is one of the most demanding ecological certification systems, awarded to products that have been conceived and designed in an ecologically intelligent way.

Certified B Corporation®

Cuento de Luz™ became a **Certified B Corporation©** in 2015. The prestigious certification is awarded to companies which use the power of business to solve social and environmental problems and meet higher standards of social and environmental performance, transparency, and accountability.

My Neighbor Frankie
Text © 2020 Ignacio Sanz
Illustrations © 2020 Eva Poyato
© 2020 Cuento de Luz SL
Calle Claveles, 10 | Urb. Monteclaro | Pozuelo de Alarcón | 28223 | Madrid | Spain
www.cuentodeluz.com
Original title in Spanish: *Mi vecino Paco*
English translation by Jon Brokenbrow
ISBN: 978-84-16733-86-6
Printed in PRC by Shanghai Cheng Printing Company March 2020, print number 1806-3

MY NEIGHBOR
FRANKIE

Ignacio Sanz   **Eva Poyato**

I have a neighbor
Whose name is Frankie.
He's kind of old,
And he walks with a stoop.

He came from South America,
All the way across the Atlantic,
Leaving behind him
Mighty rivers, tropical jungles,
Storms, and shipwrecks.

He traveled across half the world
On foot and by horse,
In trains and cars,
In boats and planes.

He worked in the circus,
And then in the theater.
He played Don Quixote,
A judge, and a soldier,
A bloodthirsty bandit,
A doctor, and a magician.
He knows more stories
Than anyone in the world.
And when he tells them to me,
I just sit there, amazed.

His house is like a menagerie.
He's got a dog and a cat,
And you should see what happens
When they get mad.
Barking and hissing,
Running round and round,
Chasing each other's tails.

He's got a talking parrot too,
Who knows tongue twisters,
Poems, and rhymes.
He says good morning in Spanish:
"¡Buenos días, Frankie!"
And sometimes–only sometimes–
He says very naughty things.

There are two turtles,
Who crawl around
From place to place.
The parrot calls them
"pesky little plodders."

And there are lots of ants
Beneath the cupboard
That carry away the leftovers,
The crumbs and the scraps.

And out on his balcony
In the middle of summer,
I once saw a lizard without a tail,
Chasing grasshoppers, crickets,
Spiders, and bugs.
Sometimes you can even hear
The croaking of a frog.

Because my neighbor Frankie
Lives all on his own,
With all of his memories,
And all of his years,
He yells and yells
When his little menagerie
Gets out of control.
That's when we hear him say
All sorts of colorful things.

From our house,
We can hear just how mad he gets.

My mom tells me not to worry,
That he's just a crazy old guy,
Who doesn't know what he's saying.
But he isn't crazy:
He's the smartest man I know.

Whenever I see him on the stairs,
He always says "Hi!"
In a big, booming voice.
   "Good morning, David!"
   "Good morning, Frankie," I say.
And he always leaves me
Some gum or some candy,
To enjoy on the steps.
He says things like,
"I wonder who could have left that there?"

And then he tells me stories
About the old days,
Back when he was young,
Brave, and daring.
He tells me about
A thousand adventures,
And we have an amazing time,
Just him and me.

One day, just like that,
He called me over, and said,
"What's that you've got there?"
And pulled a bird out of my ear.
He let it go,
And away it flew,
As I stood there, amazed.

I clapped and clapped,
And his eyes lit up
Like two lighthouses in the night.
He seemed to grow,
As if his back
Were as straight as an oak.

  "It doesn't matter, young man," he said.
"They're just magic tricks.
I've performed them a thousand times,
On the stage."

Sometimes he tells me
About the wildest dreams.
  "You know, one day
In the middle of summer,
I climbed up onto a cloud,
And I tied it up with a rope.
Then I asked it if it could rain, a little,
And it left all the gardens
Shimmering in the sunlight."

"It doesn't matter, young man," he said.
"They're just magic tricks.
I've performed them a thousand times,
On the stage."

He's a good guy,
My neighbor Frankie.
He's sentimental,
And a true artist.

Now he lives alone,
Together with his menagerie,
Seeking the love
That all of us seek.